For the real Buddy, because he is the best dog ever, and for the real Earl, even though he prickles me. — MF

For my Albert. — CS

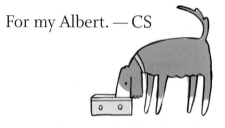

Text copyright © 2015 by Maureen Fergus
Illustrations copyright © 2015 by Carey Sookocheff
Published in Canada and the USA in 2015 by Groundwood Books

Groundwood Books / House of Anansi Press
110 Spadina Avenue, Suite 801, Toronto, Ontario M5V 2K4
or c/o Publishers Group West
1700 Fourth Street, Berkeley, CA 94710

We acknowledge for their financial support of our publishing program the Canada Council for the Arts, the Government of Canada through the Canada Book Fund (CBF) and the Ontario Arts Council.

Canada Council for the Arts   Conseil des Arts du Canada

ONTARIO ARTS COUNCIL
CONSEIL DES ARTS DE L'ONTARIO
an Ontario government agency
un organisme du gouvernement de l'Ontario

Library and Archives Canada Cataloguing in Publication
Fergus, Maureen, author
Buddy and Earl / written by Maureen Fergus ; illustrated by Carey Sookocheff.
Issued in print and electronic formats.
ISBN 978-1-55498-712-2 (bound).—ISBN 978-1-55498-713-9 (pdf)
I. Sookocheff, Carey, illustrator II. Title.
PS8611.E735B84 2015   jC813'.6   C2015-900022-X
                                                C2015-900023-8

The illustrations were done in Acryl Gouache on watercolor paper and assembled in Photoshop.
Design by Michael Solomon
Printed and bound in Malaysia

BUDDY
and
EARL

MAUREEN FERGUS

Pictures by

CAREY SOOKOCHEFF

GROUNDWOOD BOOKS
HOUSE OF ANANSI PRESS
TORONTO   BERKELEY

It was a rainy afternoon. Buddy was feeling
bored and a little lonely.

Suddenly, Meredith ran into the living room carrying a mysterious box.

Meredith put the box on the floor.

"Stay, Buddy!" she said. "I'll be right back."

Buddy concentrated hard on staying.

Then he got an itch. By the time he'd
finished scratching it, he'd forgotten all
about staying.

He trotted over and peered into the box. Inside, there was a strange-looking thing.

Buddy stared at the thing.
He wondered what it was.
He sniffed and sniffed.
  Maybe I should lick it,
he thought.

Maybe not.

All at once, the thing began to snuffle
and hiss and make funny popping sounds.
It's alive! thought Buddy. *How exciting!*

"Hello!" cried Buddy. "My name is Buddy!"

"Hello," said the thing in a muffled voice. "My name is Earl."

"I see," said Buddy. "And what are you, Earl?"

"I'm a race car," said Earl.

Buddy studied Earl carefully.

Then he said, "You do not have a steering wheel. You do not have wheels. I do not think you are a race car, Earl."

"You're right," said Earl. "I'm not a race car. I'm a giraffe."

Buddy thought about this.

Then he said, "I am pretty sure that giraffes have long, graceful necks, Earl. As far as I can tell, you have no neck at all."

"Good point," said Earl. "I'm not a giraffe.
I'm a sea urchin."

This did not seem right to Buddy, either.

"You look like a sea urchin, Earl, but I do
not think you are a sea urchin," he said. "You
see, sea urchins are underwater creatures and
the living room is not underwater."

"There's obviously no fooling you, Buddy," said Earl. "So I'm going to tell you the truth."

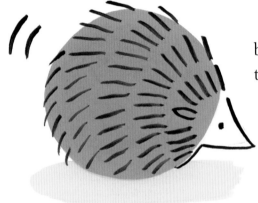

Slowly, Earl changed from a tight ball of prickles into a flattish prickly thing with a face.

"The truth is that I'm a talking hairbrush."

Buddy was almost positive that Earl was not a talking hairbrush.

Before he could give voice to his doubts, however, Earl said, "And what are you, Buddy? Wait! Don't tell me. Let me guess."

RADFORD PUBLIC LIBRARY
30 WEST MAIN STREET
RADFORD, VA 24141
540-731-3621

Earl examined Buddy from top to bottom.

"You're very tall," said Earl. "Are you a skyscraper?"

No said Buddy.

Earl examined Buddy from side to side.
"You look very strong," said Earl. "Are
you a rhinoceros?"

No said Buddy.

Earl examined Buddy from front
to back.
"You're furry with big ears and
a long tail," said Earl. "Are you a
mouse?"

No said Buddy.

"I was joking," said Earl. "I know you're not a mouse. You're a pirate, just like me."

"I am?" said Buddy.

"Yes, and that is our pirate ship," said Earl.

"That is not a pirate ship," said Buddy. "That is a couch."

"ALL HANDS ON DECK!" bellowed Earl.

"I am not allowed on the couch," said Buddy.

"Pirates can do whatever they want," said Earl. "So help me out of this box. Quick, before the sharks get me!"

Buddy did not want the sharks to get
Earl, so he helped him out of the box.
Earl climbed aboard the pirate ship.
Buddy jumped up after him.

"Uh-oh," said Earl. "We're heading into a storm."

"Uh-oh," said Buddy.

"Can you hear the wind howling, Buddy?" cried Earl.

"I can hear it, Earl!" cried Buddy.

"Can you feel the waves crashing down on us, Buddy?" shouted Earl.

"I can feel them, Earl!" shouted Buddy.

Suddenly, Earl lurched sideways.

"Oh no," he gasped. "We've hit a reef!"

"Oh no," gasped Buddy. "What's a reef?"

"We're sinking fast, Buddy!" shouted Earl. "Quick — jump onto that lifeboat!"

"That is not a lifeboat!" shouted Buddy. "That is a coffee table!"

"JUMP!" roared Earl.

Buddy jumped.

Just then, Mom walked into the room.

Buddy tried to look innocent as he slid along the deck of the lifeboat and toppled to the floor at her feet.

"What's going on here?" cried Mom.

"Don't panic, we're both fine," said Earl. "I gave orders to abandon ship."

Mom didn't seem to hear Earl.

"You know you're not allowed on the furniture, Buddy," she scolded.

"That was my fault," admitted Earl. "I told him that pirates could do whatever they wanted."

"And what have you done to poor little Earl?" asked Mom.

"He's been loyal and brave — the best first mate a pirate captain ever had," replied Earl.

"Honestly, Buddy," grumbled Mom. "Sometimes I don't know what gets into you."

Mom put Earl in his box and put the box on the kitchen table.

Then she went looking for Meredith.

After she was gone, Buddy thought about how he didn't feel bored or lonely anymore. He thought about how Earl had taken responsibility for his part in their adventure. He thought about the nice things Earl had said about him.

After he was done thinking, Buddy climbed up onto the kitchen table and looked into Earl's box.

"I think I know what you are, Earl," he said.

"What do you think I am, Buddy?" asked Earl.

"I think you are a friend," said Buddy.

"I think you are right," said Earl.